THE LOST GODS

THE LOST GODS

by Dorothy Quick

From the backwaters of the Universe came two Beings—radiant, terrible—to challenge the love of a mortal man and woman!

It seemed as though everyone entered into a conspiracy to keep me from marrying Harvey Winters. Even Harvey himself.

He asked me to be his wife in stiff, old-fashioned phraseology, almost as though it were against his will, and then before I had a chance to answer, said: "I must tell you that though I love you I am not the man you should marry. I don't think it's in me to make any woman happy because of the Dream Woman."

"The dream woman?" I exclaimed.

"All my life I've had strange dreams of a beautiful, wonderful woman. I can't describe her because her loveliness is beyond words. She comes to me in dreams. I've spent my life searching for her counterpart even though I knew such a glorious being could never be of earth. It always seems as though I'm being pulled to far away places to search for her. That's why I came to Mexico. I'll always worship her in a strange, indefinable way, but I love you, Irene, though I'm not sure I can make you happy—because of her."

I looked at him. His eyes were shining with the faraway look I had often seen in them. He had wonderful eyes, black, deeply set under straight, heavy brows. His mouth was firm, his jaws strong, his nose finely chiselled. His hair grew in blond tight curls all over his head and gave him the look of a Rubens painting.

"I'm not afraid of dreams," I said boldly.

"It's almost as though she were real." Harvey, at least, was honest.

"But she isn't, and you do love me," I exclaimed triumphantly.

I lifted my face to his and in the magic of our kiss forgot that some scientist had said, "Dreams are more real than reality until they are shown to be false."

No one was happy over my engagement, and when we announced we were going to be married as soon as the license could be procured, everyone was miserable. If I hadn't been of age my family would have forbidden the match entirely.

THE LOST GODS

"After all, we know nothing about this young man, and he is very strange. Nothing definitely odd, of course, but he's not quite like other people," my mother kept saying. And my father muttered, "If he only wasn't able to support you!"

But he was able to support me. He had an assured income of fifteen thousand dollars a year. There was nothing definitely odd as mother had said—no real reason for anyone interfering.

I have often wondered if, knowing what lay ahead, I would still have married Harvey—if I would have had the courage. I might not have been brave enough, so I'm glad that I wasn't able to look into the future. Perhaps the kindest thing God ever did for human beings was to throw a veil over what is to be, and yet, like Pandora, most people are always trying to lift that veil and unloose more trouble for themselves than Pandora let out of her box.

I didn't try to peer into the future. I was too happy in the present. As the days passed, Harvey lost a great deal of the strange detached manner that had been his and became more and more natural. We spent the time, while we waited for legal formalities to be attended to, exploring the Mexico of the Aztecs. Harvey amazed me with his knowledge of these people, their gods, and customs. I was particularly interested, for I had come to Mexico especially to see everything I could connected with the Aztecs and Mayans, as I was writing a book on Cortez and his capture of the land that was sheltering us.

When Harvey told me that he had heard of a little known temple that was four or five days' trip into the forests, and asked if I would like to go there for our honeymoon, I was enthusiastic, so Harvey set about making the arrangements.

We were married on a bright, sun-shiny day, and, after a modest wedding breakfast, set out on our excursion. Harvey drove his own car, and a second one followed with our supplies, in charge of the Mexicans we had hired to go into the forest with us. When the time came we would have to abandon the automobiles.

THE LOST GODS

For three days I knew happiness beyond my wildest dreams, a happiness so wonderful and so complete it almost made up for the misery that followed.

The fourth night we camped in the woods. I was very tired. We had ridden horseback all afternoon through the thick underbrush, ever since we had abandoned the cars on the outskirts of the forest. We made quite a procession as we struck into the interior. Our guide went first, Harvey and I followed, trailed by five husky Mexicans mounted and leading two extra horses laden with our equipment.

When I could go no further they pitched our camp among great trees that shut out every vestige of light. We sat for a while in front of our tent before we went to bed. The Mexicans had already rolled up in blankets on the ground not far away. Harvey told me legends of the Prince Quatomec who had fought the Spaniards with all the fire Montezuma lacked, and who had been betrayed and hung like a felon in this very forest, perhaps under the very tree that sheltered us. It was a weird tale for a shivery background. I was glad to go to sleep in Harvey's arms.

As I have said I was very tired but despite my fatigue. I woke up suddenly feeling as though there was some alien presence in the tent. I could hear Harvey's even breathing beside me. I didn't want to wake him, but I had to know if there were really someone—or something—in the tent. I switched on a flashlight I kept under my pillow. The the canvas walls contained nothing that had not been there when I went to sleep.

The light hit Harvey's face and when I saw it I caught my breath. He was still asleep but stamped upon his countenance was an expression of ineffable content, and even more, for added to it was a rapture beyond any I had been able to bring to his face.

I knew without telling that he was dreaming of her—that she was there. I too had felt something in the room; I felt it still.

Then all at once that feeling left me and at the same time the light died away from Harvey's face. He stirred restlessly. "Why? Why do you fr—" he muttered and then fell into a deeper, dreamless sleep.

I switched off my light, buried my head in the pillow and sobbed, my whole being racked with grief. How could I compete with anyone, dream or real, who could bring a look like that to a man's face. It was almost morning before I cried myself to sleep.

The next day I asked Harvey if he had had a dream and he said no. He said it so furtively that I would have known he lied even if I hadn't seen his beatified expression in the night. Evidently he had made up his mind not to tell me any more about his dream woman. This was an added blow and made me more miserable than ever. I would do my best to fight the dream, but having to fight deceit too made it all the harder. That night I prayed for help to conquer the dream woman and win Harvey's thoughts solely for myself.

About midnight I awoke suddenly as I done the night before. But this time, instead of an alien presence, I sensed danger!

It had been a hot night and we had left the flap of the tent open. In the dim light from the embers of the dying fire I saw Harvey bending over me. His eyes were fixed—the eyes of a sleep-walker. His right hand was raised and something bright and sharp glistened in his hand.

The innate instinct of preservation that is part of us all acted for me—I rolled aside just as the knife came flashing down.

As it buried itself in the mattress I could not prevent the scream that rose involuntarily to my lips.

The next thing I was conscious of was Harvey's puzzled voice: "Irene, Irene—where are you?" and then the voice of Juan, our Mexican guide, anxiously asking: "Señora, what is it?"

I raised myself to hide the dagger in the bed and answered the guide: "I thought I saw something but there's no one here. Will you shut the tent flap, please?"

"Si, Señora. There is no one. I will watch—fear nothing."

The opening was soon covered and Harvey lit our oil lamp. His fingers shook as he held the match.

"What was it? I heard you scream and I woke up to find myself standing by the bed."

I still hid the knife. "Did you dream, Harvey?" I asked.

This time he didn't lie, "Yes—She came to me. She wanted me to do something." I could see the effort he was making to remember. Then suddenly an expression of horror froze his face. "She wanted me to kill—you——My God! Irene, did I try—"

I moved aside so he could see the knife plunged deep into the mattress where my heart should have been.

Harvey gave one agonized look then dropped on his knees beside me, great sobs racking his body. "Irene, my darling, to think I might have—"

I soothed him as though he had been a little child frightened by the dark. After a bit he raised tortured, helpless eyes to mine. "What are we to do?"

It was plain he was panic-stricken. So was I. It was a terrible situation. I knew Harvey in his right mind would never hurt me, but a dream-ridden, sleep-walking Harvey—I was afraid, afraid for my love and for my life. The situation had grown too much for me to cope with. I felt beaten spiritually and physically. "You must sleep outside with the men until we get back to civilization and then you must see a psychologist who can cure you of your obsession. That is if you love me, Harvey. The time has come when you must choose between your Dream Woman and me."

There is no choice, Irene; you are my wife. I will do as you say." His words were all they should be but I sensed a curious withdrawal in them and I knew that the Dream Woman's hold on him was stronger than I had guessed.

"Shall we give up the temple?" he asked.

I shook my head. "We're so near now. Besides if you stay outside at night, I'll be safe.

He took me in his arms, ran his fingers through my black curls, looked into my eyes. "You are so lovely, Irene, so sweet." His lips brushed my cheek.

The triumph of the night was mine, with only the reminder of the knife tucked securely in its sheath to show how nearly it had been hers.

The temple was magnificent. When I saw it, I was glad the terror I still felt after my last night's experience hadn't kept me away. Off the beaten track, it was in an almost perfect state of preservation. We spent the morning exploring it and looking at the uncomparable carvings it contained and then had our lunch in the native village that was clustered around the foot of the elevation the temple was built upon.

The people were charming and kindly. I couldn't understand their language but through the guide I made arrangements to spend the night in one of the largest and cleanest mud huts, and engaged one of the women to stay with me as maid. She was to sleep outside the door so I felt comparatively safe. When after lunch Harvey asked if I wanted to explore the small surrounding foothills with him, I assented gladly. I had no fear of Harvey in he daytime.

We left Juan, the guide, in charge of our men, who had already made friends in the village, and started out.

After a bit it was rough going but I was used to tramping and didn't mind.

We had almost reached the summit of the hill Juan had told us commanded a wonderful view of the surrounding country when a rain-storm came up with all the suddenness of the tropics. One minute the sky was bright and clear, the next the whole world seemed wrapped in gloom through which only the flashes of lightning and distant thunder could penetrate.

"It's too late to get back. We'd better find some place to shelter," Harvey remarked as the first drops of rain began to fall.

"I thought I saw a cave a way back," I told him, little knowing that the one glimpse I had had of the hollow in the hillside was going to affect the rest of my life. If I had, I would have gone rushing down the mountain to the village—or would I? That is a question I yet can't answer.

We made our way down the hill through the spattering rain drops that fell faster as we went.

The cave was just where I remembered it and we reached it just in time, for the rain drops had become a beating downpour and the lightning was beyond anything I had ever seen.

The cave was spacious. From a narrow entrance it branched out into unexpected proportions. We went halfway in and sat down, our backs against the wall. Harvey's arm was around me and I was content, only I hoped the storm would abate before nightfall. I didn't want to stay in the cave alone with Harvey after what had happened that one night.

We were smoking cigarettes and Harvey was telling me about a storm he had seen in India, when there came a terrible crash of thunder that seemed to shake everything within a radius of miles. I could feel the wall behind us tremble. I saw a few loose stones falling in front of the cave's entrance and then, even while I was calling Harvey's attention to them, there was an ominous rumble and we were plunged into complete darkness!

Harvey pulled out his lighter and to our horror we discovered that there had been a landslide and the entrance to the cave was sealed off!

Why my hair didn't turn white in that instant I don't know.

Harvey rose splendiy to the occasion. The first thing to do was to conserve our light, he said, so he built a fire of some dead wood lying around the cave. "The air is fresh. There must be another entrance somewhere. We'll explore," Harvey said calmly.

We set out, using a lighted brand from the fire as a torch.

In the back of the cave was another pile of dirt and stone and what looked like crudely made blocks.

"I believe there was a sealed doorway here and the landslide loosened it," Harvey announced after a quick glance.

It was quite true. One could see evidences of an ancient doorway carved out of stone.

We went through and entered a series of rooms that, while of a cave-like formation, had evidently been fashioned partly by man. From time to time as we went on Harvey discarded one burning stick after another, lighting a fresh one before he stamped the last out.

At last we reached what looked like the end of our journey—a small square room. Harvey was lighting another torch so I looked about. There was something that resembled an altar at the far end, behind it some kind of picture painted on the stone wall. I could vaguely distinguish bright colors. But I could see no exit!

Was this to be the end? Immured in a cave—I felt a slow kind of horror creep over me. I was young, I wanted to live and love.

Harvey's voice, highly pitched with emotion, broke into my thoughts: "Irene—Irene, look—look at the picture?

He had moved nearer and the light from the burning wood illuminated the wall behind the altar.

It contained rather crudely done in brilliant colors, the painting of a man and woman. They had austere faces of a beauty that defies adjectives. I could mention every one in the dictionary and still not half describe the wonder of those countenances.

I could say their was reddish-gold, their skin camellia-like in its quality, their eyes like the deep purple of a violet's petal that is almost black. It would be true but it would be trite compared to the glory of that painting. They were alike, these two, and definitely above ordinary mortals. The man wore only a short length of green material around his loins, held in place by a jewel-studded belt. The woman had a similar belt girdling a green robe which left her shoulders, arms and legs bare and made no attempt to hide the classic lines of her figure. About her throat was a necklace of what look like emeralds, with one huge stone falling between her breasts. On their faces were expressions of such utter peace and calm strength that I felt as though I should kneel down to worship. I had actually started to genuflect when Harvey cried:

"It is my Dream Woman at last!"

Simultaneously with his words came again that ominous rumble. Everything began to shake and the next thing I knew it seemed, as though the whole world was in upheaval. I was knocked off my feet and flung violently on the ground. The last thing I remember was Harvey falling too, and then I knew nothing more.

*

WHEN I regained consciousness, the first thing I saw was the space where the picture had been—blue sky with the red streaks of the setting sun across it. The picture and the altar had vanished, leaving a great gap in the mountainside. I looked for Harvey. He was lying close beside me. Somewhat unsteadily I gained my feet discovering I was badly shaken but not hurt. Just as I readied Harvey he opened his eyes.

"The picture?" he gasped.

"Gone. But it has left a way open for us. I think we'd better go before something else happens." I was curt. I couldn't help recalling what he had said before the upheaval hit us.

He groaned. "To think such beauty is destroyed."

As I remember those two beautiful faces, I agreed it was sacrilege but in my inmost heart I was glad. I hadn't yet stopped to figure out how finding the actual representation of his Dream Woman was going to affect our future. I only wanted to get away from the cave.

"Do you see green glittering there?" Harvey asked, pointing. He was on his feet now and I saw his forehead had a cut on it. I tied his handkerchief around it, and it and then followed the direction of his finger.

Where the altar had been there was something green shining.

"Perhaps it's part of the picture. We must save it if we can," Harvey said.

Together we walked over. There was nothing but debris everywhere in this part of the cave but in a hollowed-out section of the ground was a mound of green. I bent down and my fingers touched something cold and hard. I lifted it and discovered I had in my hands the necklace the woman in the picture had worn. Or its counterpart. The stones were uncut emeralds, strung on a gold chain which was knotted in between the stones.

"Her necklace! Irene, do you realize the significance of that? The painting was an actual person. She isn't a dream woman. She's real." I had never seen Harvey so excited.

"She was, you mean." I slipped the necklace over my head. The cool stone caressed my skin. "It's a lovely necklace."

"There's something else there." Harvey leaned over. When he straightened up he held the two belts of the picture in his hands. Made of heavy gold they were thickly entrusted with the gleaming emeralds.

He held up the smaller one. "To think this once touched her? He was like an East Indian devotee who had hypnotized himself.

I felt I must keep to sanity. "Let's hope it's not too small for me." I was matter-of-fact. "These stones, if genuine, must be worth a fortune and I'm sure they are real considering the picture and the ancient look of the altar."

Harvey caught hold of himself. "That was not Aztec work. There was no sign of leathered serpents or any of their symbols. It must have been even older. You are right. We must hide our find. The Mexicans might rob us or the government put in a claim." He handed me the smaller belt. I slipped it on underneath the sweater I wore over my riding breechs. Harvey did likewise with the larger one. Then I put the necklace under the sweater and taking off the bandanna I wore on my head tied it around my neck so the stones would not be seen.

We searched in the hollow but there was nothing more except some decayed bits of leather, remains of the bag that had held the jewels, probaly. We kicked some loose dirt down in the hollow and then climbed out over the debris into the open air. Nothing ever felt so wonderful as the rush of it against me when I finally stepped out on the mountainside.

Harvey poked around to see if he could find a fragment of the picture, but there was nothing, only powdered dust.

"If I could only have preserved her face," he half moaned.

"Then you should have kept her husband's too. Can't you see they were mated, those two glorious beings? Oh, Harvey, forget her—let us be happy together." Even as I said the words, I recognized the futility of what I was urging. I could never forget those faces and I had only seen them once whereas Harvey had been seeing the Dream Woman for years. The outlook for me was pretty bad. Only one thing I could not reconcile—the thought of murder with that pure, austere beauty. Yet she had bidden Harvey kill me. Would she again? What did our finding the picture and the jewels represent? I would have given everything I possessed-except Harvey—to know the answer.

Halfway down the mountain we met Juan and some of our escort. Juan kissed our hands solemnly and after rejoicing over our safety, said: "Ah, Seõor, Seõora, we feared for you when the Lost Gods spoke."

*

TWO words picked themselves out in my brain. "Lost Gods?" "Si Senõra,

14

the Gods of the far far past beyond the knowledge of man, they who ruled the lightnings and dreams." Juan was quite serious.

Harvey started. "Tell us more Juan."

The Mexican made an odd sign with his hand. "We talk little of the Lost Gods Senōr; few except the very old keep their memory green against the time when they shall come again."

"Come again?" Once more I echoed his words.

"My great grandfather knows the legend. The Gods—a man-God and the Woman his mate—ruled the world. Something happened that displeaed the man-God. What, no one remembers, for it is too far back into the past. The man-God laid waste the land with his lightning and then took his wife away from earth. But he promised to come back again at the proper time and left a link to earth to make a way back."

"How could he?" I asked although I knew the answer.

"He left his mortal attributes and hers—magic stones set in gold, with their likeness in some secret place. When the time comes, they will be found and then the finder will open the road." Juan's face had the mystical expression that only the superstitious ever have.

The necklace lay heavy against me. "But, Juan," I protested, "That's stupid. Suppose anyone did find the magic stones. They wouldn't know what to do to open the way."

Juan smiled pityingly at my ignorance. "Did I not say the Lost God was the master of dreams, Señora? Whoever finds the stones and wears them through the night will be instructed. But they have been hidden hundreds of years, beyond the reach of time; they will not be found in our life, lady." His white teeth flashed as he laughed at his own joke.

He little knew! I could tell by Harvey's rapt expression he believed every word. As for me my thoughts were in chaos. I could not find my way out. Only one thing I knew that at night I would sleep with the necklace about my neck and the girdle around my waist. I followed out my resolution but nothing happened—nothing. I slept a deep, dreamless sleep and had the first really good night I had had since I saw Harvey dreaming of the Lost Goddess-

—to give the Dream Woman her proper title.

Harvey entered the mud hut as I finished my breakfast.

One look at him and I knew something unusual had happened. He was seething with excitement.

"Irene, it's all true," he exclaimed. "Every word Juan said. Last night I dreamed—not of her"—the way he said the pronoun made me crawl with jealousy—"but of him, the Lost God. He came to me and told me what to do. You must help me, Irene. Think how wonderful it will be to see those shining ones in the flesh—to bring them back to rule the world!"

"I like the world as it is—Oh, Harvey!" I caught his hands. "Can't we forget all this? It's an ordinary legend and it's preyed on your mind to the extent you did dream of him but that doesn't mean there's truth, in the dream or the story. It's too utterly fantastic."

"The picture and the jewels were real."

He had me there.

"Don't you see, Irene? This is my mission in life. What I was born for—to be the opener of the way. That's why I've always dreamed of her. I understand now why I have been a man tortured and divided by loving two women. It was to spur me on. I will always worship the Lost Goddess but it is you that I really love. I know mortals cannot mate with Gods. But I can serve her; so can you. We can worship them together—will you, Irene?"

"Yes, Harvey," I heard myself saying. I could never resist the pleading in his voice. I didn't remind him that his Goddess had urged him to kill me, because I had decided in one swift moment I would rather die than go on sharing Harvey with her. Besides if he did as his dreams commanded and nothing happened the ghost would be laid. And if the Gods materialized I had faith in the man-God to manage his wife. The Lost God's face had haunted me ever since I had seen it pictured on the wall. It had drawn me with a strange fascination that I struggled against and even now would not admit. I loved Harvey but my heart beat faster at the thought of actually seeing the Lost God.

Somehow I was no longer afraid.

THE LOST GODS

*

We got back to Mexico City without any further happening worth recording.

Harvey continued to dream. Each night the God came to him and gave him instruction as to what he was to do, all of which Harvey wrote down and kept from me. To my great satisfaction the Goddess didn't ever figure in his dreams. Nor did he seem to miss her presence. I began to hope. We motored back with the family and the Mexican custom officers little suspected the precious antiques we were smuggling out of their country, which we hid under the hood of our car.

We settled in our new house on father's estate at Locust Valley. Harvey took two emeralds from the girdle of the Goddess which I still wore, and sold them for a fabulous sum on the Dream God's instructions. What the other stones and the necklace would be worth was almost beyond comprehension. With part of the money Harvey bought land on the occan front between Southampton and Quogue. Ostensibly he began to build a summer home. Only he and I knew it was a home for the Lost Gods, built entirely on their specifications. I was not to see it until it was ready for Harvey and I to perform the last final ceremony for the opening of the way.

Harvey was calmer and less mystical than I had ever seen him. He clung to me and we were quite happy. By tacit consent we occupied diffcrent rooms at night. I was no longer afraid but I saw no use in taking chances.

I even went so far as to consult an eminent brain specialist who was an old family friend. I had had my dark moments of doubt as to Harvey's sanity, but after observing him, Dr. Harlow said he was perfectly sane. "It's the long arm of coincidence," he reassured me. "Harvey dreamt of a woman, probably a fixation from some childish experience. When he saw the picture he immediately invested it with the personality of this dream woman, and after hearing the legend, his sensitive mind transferred his dreams from the woman to the man. Let him go ahead with his experiment—nothing will come of it. But you will have peace afterward plus a summer home and a fortune in jewels."

THE LOST GODS

This contented me. It was my own reasoning and there was no one to point out how terribly wrong we both were.

*

Everything was prepared and ready the week before Christmas, so Harvey and I left for Southampton in his new Rolls Royce. He had of course gotten the best of everything for the God's use when they appeared. We promised the family, who had grown much attached to Harvey by now, we would be back in plenty of time for Christmas and they waved us off, little knowing what lay at the end of our road.

Harvey drove at a tremendous rate of speed. "There is much to do wlen we arrive," he explained, and added: "He was particular about the time."

I couldn't help the thought that if it hadn't been for Doctor Harlow I should have considered myself mad to go with Harvey—a Harvey who had always been strange, who had tried to kill me once and might again with some unholy rite in the God's service. But I had long ago made up my mind I would rather die than continue as we were and I firmly believed nothing would happen. Besides if it did, if the Shining Beings materialized, I had faith in the Lost God.

We tore through the sleepy town of Southampton until we left the houses with lights in them behind us and reached the ocean road where the untenanted homes of the summer people loomed darkly. I had never been there except when the summmer colony was in residence. The end of December found this part of Southampton a deserted village. The huge empty houses looked strangely sinister and forbidding on the cold twilight. As we rode on and on they became fewer and farther apart until at last there were none at all, only the dunes stretching down to the ocean on one side, and on the other the long green marches running toward Shinnecock Bay.

There was no sign of life anywhere except an occasional wheeling gull against the gray sky. I had never thought that part of Long Island could be sinister but it was.

All at once we turned in between two heavy wooden gates set in a high stone wall. "This is the place I built according to the Gods' instructions."

THE LOST GODS

Harvey broke the long silence and the sound of his voice was a relief.

At the same moment I saw the house, a strange modernistic looking affair which had an afinity with the houses of ancient Egypt in the huge pylons either side of the bronze doors. Harvey left the car in a garage near the gate and we walked up the long drive to the house. Then Harvey took me inside a corridor and let me look into the central room which really was the house. It was huge, two stories high, with a glass ceiling through which one could see the sky. The wall facing the ocean was glass too, crystal clear. In the dim light I could still distinguish the waves leaping upon the shore below.

The other walls were hung with damask of a soft indefinite shade of ice green. There was a velvet couch at the center of the long wall and before it something that looked exactly like the altar in the cave.

The rest of the room contained little furniture—an oddly carved chest and a few chairs. The floor was covered with a thick green carpet of the same illusive shade as the walls.

I saw all this in the second that Harvey pulled aside the damask drapery for me to look. Then he let it fall to again, shutting the room off. "We cannot enter there now," he said firmly.

The house was odd enough. The big room was its core. Around it ran a corridor six feet wide from which other rooms opened, enclosing the whole in a big square. Harvey showed me to a very pretty bedroom which had a modern bathroom attached.

On a chair was laid a pile of green chiffon. Harvey pointed to it. "If you'll rest an hour and then put this on, we can go back to the big room and wait the time."

I might have been a stranger for there was no personal touch in Harvey's tones. I nodded and he left telling me he would call me in time. I couldn't rest. I lay on the bed thinking of Harvey utterly obsessed with a pictured face, and of myself too, for I could see the Lost God's features line for line. I wished the Gods would come long enough to free us from this obsession and then return to the starry spaces.

I felt strangely keyed up and my mind darted hither and thither like a restless swallow until I could not focus it on any subject.

It was a relief to hear Harvey's knock on the door and his, "Hurry, it is nearly time!"

I called out that I would. Harvey didn't come in so I struggled into the garment he had left on the chair. It was patterned after the robe of the Lost Godess, made of several layers of various coloured green chiffons. I slipped it over my head and fastened it around my waist with Her girdle. The necklace was already on my neck, the necklace which She had worn. As a last touch I put my feet into odd looking sandals of gilded leather.

Then I looked at myself in the long mirror set into the door.

The strange costume was becoming. Through the layers of chiffon I could glimpse the flesh tones of my skin. My bare legs were straight and slim. I looked like a temple neophyte with my black curls clustering about my face. I had not the radiant beauty of the Goddess but at least I wouldn't shame Harvey.

Slowly I went out into the corridor. Harvey was waiting—a Harvey who looked handsomer than I had ever seen him. He wore a short length of green material wrapped around his hips, held at his waist with the jeweled girdle. It fell to a point a little above his knees. His legs were straight and firm, his physique marvelous. I found myself wishing that we could forget this foolishness of Lost Gods and think only of ourselves. As Harveey surveyed me, I was glad my figure was fine enough to stand the revelations of the close clinging garment he had given me to wear. He took my hand and led me along the corridor. My heart beat faster as we went.

I had made up my mind to humor him, come what would. If nothing happened, then I meant to claim him as my own. It vas a lucky thing I could not foresee how I would claim him nor what would happen when I did.

Harvey opened a thich heavy door in the corridor and pulled aside folds of green damask for me. I entered the big room.

As I did so, I heard the clang of the great door shutting behind us and when I looked back Harvey stood beside me and the wall entirely green damask. I couldn't distinguish where the material that covered the door parted.

The room was slightly different. Great ecclesiastical candles in bronze holders burned on either side of lhe altar-like table and lit the room in an eery fashion.

Before the altar was a low bowl in which incense was burning and encompassing the whole thing, altar, brazier, candles and all was a large circle made of strips of gold. Outside of that were inverted golden triangles and then another circle encompassing the first. How Harvey had managed to get so much gold at a time when gold was so scarce I didn't know.

"Now," Harvey said firmly, "put the necklace and the girdle on the altar as I do. Then come back and stand between the outer and inner circle. No matter what happens, do not cross the inside circle again for it would mean death to any but the Gods."

I put my hands up to lift the necklace over my head. I hated to part with the lovely thing. It had been my constant companion, and I had grown fond of it. Still I felt I was not being separated from it for long so I laid it upon the altar and then unclasped the girdle and placed it beside the necklace. Harvey at the same time put his belt beside mine on the altar and I noticed that he had had another belt underneath.

He uttered some strange cabalistic words in a tongue I did not understand and then motioned me to go back to my place between the golden rings. As I went he followed me. We stood inside the two circles, Harvey opposite one candelabrum while I faced the other.

Then Harvey leaned forward and, with unerring aim, threw something he took out of his belt into the bowl. A soft swirling smoke rose from it, almost like sea mist. It billowed around the inner circle and gradually spread to the other one, until it enveloped Harvey and me. I could no longer see the strange, mystical passes that Harvey was making with his hands, but I could hear his voice intoning unfamiliar words And beyond his voice the sound of the sea pounding on the shore—a deep, minor undertone that had a rhythmic quality.

I forgot everything but the solemnity of the occasion and the mist from the bowl caressed me as though it were composed of soft human fingers dipped in perfume.

All at once I felt as though the mist, the sea, and I were all fused together. As though I were a part of them, that I was above and beyond myself.

A shudder passed over my body that was almost cataclysmic. Then I felt something alien taking possession of me. It was as though an essence was being poured into my soul, as though some part of me that had always been lacking had come home. A strange power surged through me. I felt attuned to nature. Even more, I was part of nature. I knew all her secrets. Suddenly I knew I was more than human—I was a Goddess—The Lost Goddess.

Now I understood what Harvey was saying: "By the power of the word, the unmentionable word which I have spoken, I call you back from the far places. O Gods that were lost, by your promise to come again I invoke your presence!"

The words were in a strange, archaic tongue but I knew their meaning. I knew the word too, the unmentionable word. It was a part of me. Perhaps I was dreaming but—something impelled me to move forward. The mist parted to let me pass, I slipped into the inner circle. I crossed the line and I still lived. Then I knew it was no dream. I was truly the Goddess. I took the necklace and drew it over my head until it hung about my neck and the large emerald rested between my breasts. I put on the girdle and as I did so the mist bowed low before me and died away.

In the outer circle Harvey was kneeling. As I looked at him I knew the past and the present, knew that far back beyond the minds of men I had loved him and because a Goddess cannot love a human I had been taken from earth by the jealous God who loved me. Knew that I had put off my Godhead to come back to earth to find my lover age after age and that as Irene I had found him and won him. But he had in his soul remembered the Goddess he had loved in the past and he had gone to find her and as things were ordained discovered the one thing that could bring her back. Now he had called my Godhead to life again and fused together the twin parts. I was a woman and a Goddess, and both woman and Godess loved him. Strange that

I never guessed.

"Harvey!" I called and my ears hardly knew my own voice, it had become so mellow and lovely. "Harvey, my love"

He looked up. "Most glorious!" he cried, then more puzzled: "Irene—Irene, are you—you are the Lost Goddess!"

I wish I could have seen myself at that moment.

I smiled at him and my smile promised all things. "Come to me, my beloved."

He started forward. As he came I caught a reflection of myself in the copper bowl and saw that I was beautiful with an unreal brilliance that was indescribable. I was still human enough to be pleased and to relish the homage in Harvey's eyes.

"It is true. You are the Goddess. No wonder I loved you," Harvey cried.

"Come my beloved, come!" I stretched out my arms to him.

He stumbled across the inner circle and into my arms.

"To touch you—" he whispered, "to see your face—"

I clasped him in my arms. I pressed my lips to his and kissed him. It was a wonderful kiss, the perfect reunion of two lovers, separated for eons. But as it ended I felt him go limp in my arms. I lowered him to the floor and bent closer to him. He lay white and still and the awful truth came to me. The force that was in me had killed my lover! Gods and humans cannot mate, or even kiss.

As this agonizing knowledge came to me I heard a low laugh and a new voice beat on my ears: "At last—at last!"

I had forgotttn the Lost God!

There he stood in the inner circle on the other side of Harvey's prostrate body fastening the belt around his waist. Tall, majestic, with the same unearthly beauty that I possessed illuminating his countenance. But his was the cold beauty of a statue. There was no warm, pulsing humanity to temper it. I wondered how I could ever have been drawn to him even in my thoughts.

"So we meet again, my Goddess," he said, "and I owe the meeting to your lover." He touched Harvey's inanimate body with his foot.

I straightened up. "Stop or I will send you back whence you came!"

It must have been no idle threat for I saw him pause. "We will go back together," he said, "there is nothing in this cold, bleak world to hold us. We should never have left it for it was better in the old days. But I had to take you from him. I was wrong then. I should have annihilated him but I didn't know a Goddess would stoop to put aside her Godhead for a creature such as this." He looked at Harvey again.

"I loved him then, I love him now," I said simply. "You were cruel, you still are, Eater of Blood. My hate for you surives."

"He is lost to you now. You have repaid his love with death. A kindly death with your lips on his. I should be jealous but I am not. Come, we waste time. Ever since you left me I have schemed to find you but I couldn't mate with mortal. You had to resume your Godhead before you could be mine again, or leave the mortal body you had selected. That fool played into my hands. I sent him dreams from the time he was born again. He found you as I knew he would. I tried to make him kill your mortal frame and send you back to the Outer Space and me, but you prevented that. Your Godhead watched over you, for you had only put it aside. So I had to make him bring your Codhead back to the body you chose. I did my work well. And you played into my hands.

"Now he is finished, and you are mine once more!" He smiled coldly and stretched out his hand.

I knew to what he would take me. Being a Goddess I knew all things. Once before in the dim, legendary past I had fought with him and lost because his power was as strong as mine and he was wiser. But now to my Godhead was added human wisdom and love.

A line came to me: "A God is as real as the belief of his worshippers." Harvey's belief was a weapon in my hand. It was I he had worshipped in his heart, not the Lost God, and I had drawn Harvey's strength into me with that death-dealing kiss.

I bent over. I lifted Harvey in my arms as easily as though he had been a child instead of a man, for my strength was superhuman. I held him against my hip with one arm and standing thus faced the Lost God.

"No!" I cried, my voice ringing with awe-inspiring power. "No, if I must I will renounce my Godhead forever, but before I do, I will send you back, back to the far spaces, from which never again will a worshipper draw you hence!"

"So once more we struggle!" His voice matched mine. "So be it. "This time I will win forever."

He raised his hands and let loose the forces of nature. A storm arose such as I have never heard. The ocean lashed, peal after peal of thunder shook the room, lightning flashed all about us.

"Go—" I cried again. "No one has faith in you, not even I!"

I saw him fall back and then I exerted every atom of the power that I possessed. "Go, my Godhead," I shouted above the storm. "Go forever and take him with you."

I felt as though something were tearing through my being. There was a terrific wrench, a cataclysmic shudder as though some vital thing were being forced from me. At the same time came a clap of thunder and an awful streak of lightning.

*

In it I saw the Lost God, saw the reproach and defeat on his face. Then he was gone and I was Irene again. Plain Irene, no longer a Goddess but a human girl trying to hold up the insupportable weight Harvey had become. The moment I realized this I saw that behind me the green damask was in flames.

Now indeed I regretted my lost Godhead. I dragged Harvey over to where I thought the door would be.

After agonizing moments, while the flames leaped higher and crept nearer to me I found the door. I got Harvey out into the corridor away from the house, down the hill to the garage. A little superhuman strength must have been left to me for somehow or other I got him into the car.

Fortunately the key was in it and I could drive. As I went through the gates

THE LOST GODS

I looked back. The house on the Dunes was a mass of flame.

Why, believing as I did Harvey was dead, I went directly to a doctor in the village, I don't know, but I did and the doctor said Harvey had been struck by lightning. He applied first aid, and after working on him for hours, brought him bck to life.

I shall never forget the moment when Harvey's eyes opened, looked into mine, and his voice murmured weakly: "My love!"

We stayed what was left of that night with the doctor. I explained our fantastic costumes by saying we'd been to a fancy dress party, up on the Island and had just returned to Harvey's house when it was struck by lightning.

By then of course the whole town knew of the fire.

"Likely the same bolt that struck your husband," the doctor said. "Never heard of a thunder storm before, this time of the year; strange unseasonable weather."

Only Harvey and I knew there had been no lightning when he had been smitten, only the burning force that had been in me.

The doctor and his wife fixed us up a with clothes and we left the next day for Locust Valley. I still wore the emerald necklace but the girdle reposed in Harvey's pocket. The other had gone with the God. As we crossed the bridge over Shinnecock Bay, Harvey pulled over to the rail, looked down at the water below, and took out the girdle. "Shall I?" he asked, holding it poised in the window.

I looked at its unearthly beauty and then nodded. A quick throw and it was gone—far below the swirling waters.

I took off the necklace, detached the hanging stone and then gave it to Harvey. "The one stone I will keep but the rest must go." While we held these things there was always danger. They were the last link with my Godhead, and we could not keep them for fear they might prove once more a pathway.

"It's gone!" Harvey said. There was no regret in his voice, though he had thrown away a fortune. I put my hand in his.

THE LOST GODS

"Are you happy, Harvey?"

"Happier than I dreamed," Harvey smiled. "I have my Goddess and my love, and they are both one."

I looked at him and knew I had no regrets for my lost Godhead. I would never be a Goddess again, but I would live and die with the man I loved.

Harvey leaned over and our lips met. And that instant I knew that my life really began.

www.ingramcontent.com/pod-product-compliance
Lightning Source LLC
Chambersburg PA
CBHW030529130626
46549CB00007B/3163